SCOUT

PUBLISHED BY SLEEPING BEAR PRESS™

Words and Pictures by Gordon McMillan

OUT

To my
friends and family,
whose support has seen me
through the challenges that life has
brought. Thank you for all the love.
—Gordon

Text and Illustration Copyright © 2012 Gordon McMillan • All rights reserved. No part of this book may be reproduced in any manner without the express written consent of the publisher, except in the case of brief excerpts in critical reviews and articles. All inquiries should be addressed to: Sleeping Bear Press™ • 315 East Eisenhower Parkway, Suite 200 • Ann Arbor, MI 48108 • www.sleepingbearpress.com • © Sleeping Bear Press, a part of Cengage Learning. • Printed and bound in China • 10 9 8 7 6 5 4 3 2 1 • Library of Congress Cataloging-in-Publication Data • McMillan, Gordon, 1984- • Scout / written and illustrated by Gordon McMillan. • p. cm. • Summary: Scout, a Scottish terrier, has lost his favorite red ball and as he searches his tall building for it, he make friends with Cleo the cat, Frankie the fish, Harvey the hamster, and Mac the mouse. • ISBN 978-1-58536-797-9 • [1. Lost and found possessions--Fiction. 2. Balls (Sporting goods)--Fiction. 3. Scottish terrier--Fiction 4. Dogs--Fiction. 5. • Animals--Fiction.] I. Title. • PZ7.M4787822Sco 2012 • [E]--dc23 • 2012006088

Printed by China Translation & Printing Services Limited, Guangdong Province, China. 1st printing. 06/2012

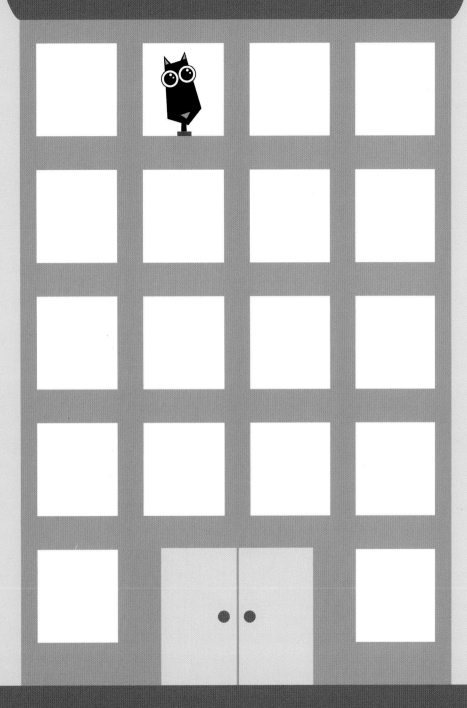

Scout lived on the top floor of a tall building.

One day he lost his
favorite shiny, red ball.

He went from

floor to floor

to look for it.

On his way he met a cat named Cleo.

"Have you seen my ball?" asked Scout. "It is shiny and red and can bounce higher than anything else."

"Nonsense!" said Cleo.
"You will see that I can
bounce higher after
we find your ball."

Scout and Cleo met a fish named Frankie.

"Have you seen my ball?"
asked Scout. "It is shiny
and red and rounder
than anything else."

"Poppycock!" said Frankie. "You will see that my bowl is rounder after we find your ball."

Then they met a hamster named Harvey.

"Have you seen my ball?" asked Scout. "It is shiny and red and can go faster than anything else."

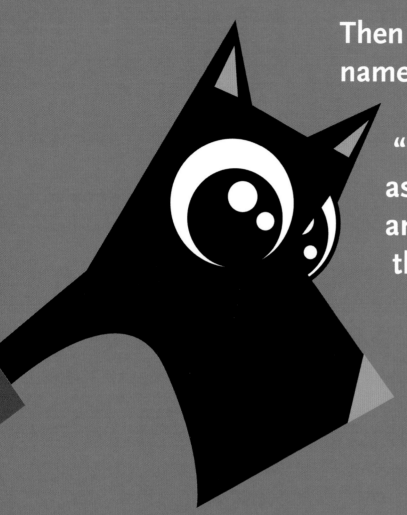

"Impossible!" said Harvey. "You will see that I can run faster after we find your ball."

They went from

floor to floor

to look for it.

They looked high
and low.

But Scout began to worry that he would never find his shiny, **red** ball. How would he show his friends what his ball could do?

Then they heard
a tiny squeak.

A gray mouse was trying to sneak away

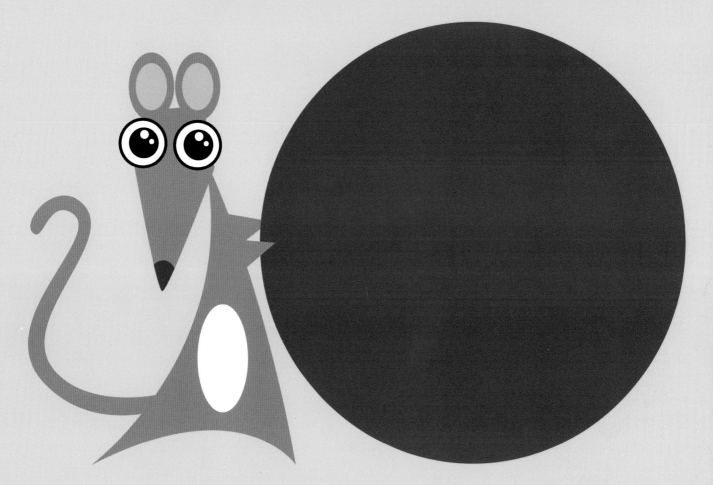

with the shiny, red ball!

They gave chase.

The little mouse teased them...

Only to crash into a wall.

Scout, Cleo, Frankie, and Harvey towered over him.
"Who are you?" demanded Scout.
"And why did you take my ball?"

"My name is Mac," said the mouse.
"And what do you mean *ball*?
I took this cheese with a red rind that you never ate."

"But it is not cheese.
Taste it and see," said Scout.

Mac took a bite. "That is horrible!"

"That is because it is meant for playing, not for eating," said Scout.

"Let me show you what I mean."

Scout bounced the ball
so high that not even
Cleo could reach it.

He balanced the ball so perfectly that not even Frankie could say his bowl was rounder.

He rolled the ball so fast that not even Harvey could keep up with it.

"That is definitely not cheese!" Mac admitted.

"What cheese could do such amazing things?"

Mac joined their fun

and the new friends played the day away

with the shiny, red ball.

They threw the ball back and forth.

They danced with the ball.

They juggled the ball.

"Good night!" they said to each other,
returning to their homes.

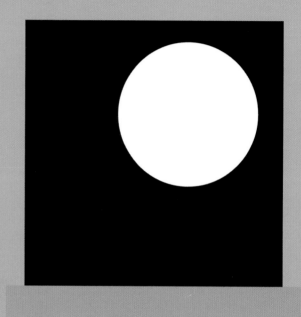

Near an open window, Scout quickly fell asleep with the ball close by his side.

As he slept, a little bat
landed on the windowsill.

"You do know that ball is meant for playing, not for eating?" said Scout.

The End.